Exploring
BEYOND THE
SOLAR SYSTEM

Nancy Dickmann

rosen publishing's
rosen central

New York

Published in 2016 by The Rosen Publishing Group, Inc.
29 East 21st Street
New York, NY 10010

First Edition

Produced for Rosen by Calcium
Editors for Calcium: Sarah Eason and Jennifer Sanderson
Designer: Greg Tucker
Consultant: David Hawksett

Photo credits: Cover © Shutterstock/Vladimir Arndt; p. 8 © NASA/JPL-Caltech; p. 10 courtesy of Wikimedia Commons/Loon, J. van (Johannes); p. 11 courtesy of Wikimedia Commons; p. 12–13 courtesy of NASA/SDO; p. 13 courtesy of NASA/Goddard; p. 14 courtesy of NASA, ESA, and the Hubble SM4 ERO Team; p. 15 © Shutterstock/Yuriy Kulik; p. 16 courtesy of NASA/Tom Tschida; p. 17 courtesy of ESA; p. 18 courtesy of NASA/STScI Digitized Sky Survey/Noel Carboni; p. 19 courtesy of NASA/JPL-Caltech; p. 20 courtesy of NASA/JPL-Caltech/UCLA; p.21 top courtesy of NASA/JPL-Caltech; p. 21 bottom courtesy of NASA/CXC; p. 22 courtesy of NASA/CXC/IAFE/G.Dubner et al & ESA/XMM-Newton; pp. 22–23 courtesy of NASA/JPL-Caltech; p. 23 © Shutterstock/IrinaK; pp. 24–25 © Dreamstime/Neutronman; p. 25 courtesy of NASA, ESA; G. Illingworth, D. Magee, and P. Oesch, University of California, Santa Cruz; R. Bouwens, Leiden University; and the HUDF09 Team; p. 26 top courtesy of Dreamstime/Creativemarc; p. 26 bottom courtesy of ESA/Hubble & NASA; p. 28 © Wikimedia Commons/Oren Jack Turner; p. 29 courtesy of NASA/CXC/M. Weiss; p. 30 © Shutterstock/catwalker; p. 31 courtesy of ESA and the Planck Collaboration; pp. 32–33 courtesy of NASA; p. 34 courtesy of ESA/Hubble & NASA; p. 35 © Dreamstime/Pseudolongino; p. 36 courtesy of NASA, ESA, M.J. Jee and H. Ford (Johns Hopkins University); p. 37 top © Dreamstime/Thomas Jurkowski; p. 37 bottom courtesy of NASA; p. 38 © Wikimedia Commons/Amble; p. 40 © Shutterstock/Paulo Afonso; p. 42 courtesy of NASA/JPL-Caltech; p. 43 courtesy of NASA Ames/SETI Institute/JPL-Caltech; p. 44 courtesy of NASA; p. 45 courtesy of NASA/JPL-Caltech/STScI.

Library of Congress Cataloging-in-Publication Data

Dickmann, Nancy, author.
Exploring beyond the solar system/Nancy Dickmann.—First edition.
    pages cm.—(Spectacular space science)
Includes bibliographical references and index.
ISBN 978-1-4994-3641-9 (library bound)—ISBN 978-1-4994-3643-3 (pbk.)—ISBN 978-1-4994-3644-0 (6-pack)
1. Stars—Juvenile literature. 2. Galaxies—Juvenile literature. 3. Solar system—Juvenile literature. 4. Outer space—Exploration—Juvenile literature. I. Title.
QB801.7.D53 2016
523.8—dc23
                                                            2014044948

Manufactured in the United States of America

CONTENTS

Chapter One

WATCHING THE SKIES

Until about 150 years ago, when gas and electricity lit up our cities, the night skies formed a twinkling blanket over Earth. Compared to the dozens of stars visible to city dwellers today, people long ago would have seen thousands of stars dancing across the sky on a clear night. However, for centuries, they were unaware of the true nature of stars and galaxies.

Most ancient cultures made a link between the objects in the sky and their religion. Stars and planets were identified with gods and goddesses, with stories told to explain their movement. People looked for patterns in the stars and named them after heroes and creatures from myths and legends. For example, one constellation represented the hunter Orion to the ancient Greeks. In their stories, he was killed by a giant scorpion. The constellation Scorpius seems to chase Orion across the sky, just as the creature did in the myth.

Ancient peoples did not just make up stories about the objects in the sky. They carefully watched and recorded their movements, using them to find their way and to mark the passage of the year. They also hoped to find out what might happen in the future. They believed that the stars could influence conditions on Earth, for example, by causing rain, drought, and plagues.

To the ancients, the skies were full of mysteries. Phenomena such as comets, meteors, and supernovae were unexpected and often frightening. Historians think that some legends of natural disasters and other catastrophes might be based on real events, such as a comet or meteorite impact.

Some ancient monuments, such as Stonehenge in Wiltshire, England, were designed to align with the sun's path through the sky.

SEVEN SISTERS

The Pleiades is a cluster of stars that is named for the seven daughters of Atlas and Pleione. A story says that Orion, the hunter, fell in love with them and chased them, until the god Zeus turned them into doves so they could escape. They flew up into the sky, where they are still seen today.

The study of the skies was an important part of life for thousands of years.

5

Constellations

Astronomers today divide the sky into eighty-eight clearly defined segments known as constellations. Many of these, like Cassiopeia, are based on constellations known since ancient times. Some of the oldest constellations are the twelve that make up the zodiac, including Gemini, Taurus, and Sagittarius. These make up a system that probably dates back to the Babylonian astronomers of nearly three thousand years ago. The twelve constellations form a circle around the ecliptic, and their positions can be used as a way of navigating. Many different ancient cultures have used the zodiac.

The astronomer Ptolemy (c. 100—c. 170 CE) was one of the first to try to formalize the constellations. His book, the *Almagest*, described forty-eight constellations that are still used by astronomers today. However, he had a problem: he could not see the whole sky. Different constellations are visible in the Northern and Southern Hemispheres. For example, someone in New York will never be able to see the constellation Crux, better known as the Southern Cross. Likewise, a person in southern Australia will only rarely see Ursa Major.

The Big Dipper is a familiar sight in the sky.

WHAT'S IN A NAME?

Many of the most familiar patterns in the night sky are actually asterisms, not constellations. An asterism is a grouping of stars that seems to form a pattern or picture when viewed from Earth. Most of them are part of larger constellations. For example, the "Big Dipper" is an asterism that is part of the larger constellation, Ursa Major.

Taurus is one of the constellations of the zodiac. It gets its name because its shape reminds people of a bull.

Soon after Ptolemy, Islamic astronomers were able to expand the catalog of constellations with their own observations of stars. They took careful notes of their positions, brightness, and color. Their work was so influential that many of the brightest stars, such as Rigel, Aldebaran, and Betelgeuse, are still referred to by their Arabic names.

Still more constellations were defined in the seventeenth and eighteenth centuries. Many of these are seen only in the Southern Hemisphere and had not been visible to the Chinese, Greeks, or Arabs. Explorers such as Pieter Keyser (1540–1596) and Frederick de Houtman (1571–1627) mapped the southern skies while sailing on trading voyages.

The Milky Way

All of the stars we see in the constellations are part of our galaxy, called the Milky Way. If you live in a city, you may not have seen the Milky Way, but if you go somewhere without too much light pollution you will see a dim, glowing band arching across the night sky. The earliest observers disagreed as to what the Milky Way actually was. Some suspected that it was made up of stars, but others, such as the Greek philosopher Aristotle (384–322 BCE), thought that it was caused by the ignition of "exhalations" from stars.

Telescopes were invented in the early seventeenth century, and the Italian astronomer Galileo (1564–1642) soon discovered that the milky band in the sky was actually made up of a huge number of stars. Nearly 150 years later, Immanuel Kant (1724–1804) theorized that the Milky Way might be a flat, rotating disc made up of millions of stars. He was right: the reason it appears as a band across the sky is that we are observing it from our position inside the disc.

In the last century, we have learned much more about our own galaxy. It contains between 100 and 400 billion stars, arranged in a shape called a barred spiral. Our sun (and the solar system that surrounds it) is located on one of the arms of the spiral, called the Orion Arm. The entire Milky Way is about 100,000 light years in diameter.

The sun

Our sun is about twenty-seven thousand light years from the center of the Milky Way.

MILK IN THE SKY?

The Milky Way is so-named because it forms a white band across the sky, like spilled milk. "Milky Way" is a direct translation of the Roman name for it, Via Lactea. The Romans took their name from the ancient Greek version, Galaktikos Kyklos. In fact, our word "galaxy" is based on the Greek name for the Milky Way. Some cultures know it by different names; for example, to the Chinese it is the "Silver River."

In its brightest parts, the stars of the Milky Way are clustered far too closely to discern individual points of light.

9

Earth at the Center?

For a very long time, most people believed that Earth was the center of the universe. It makes sense if you try to put yourself in the shoes of people who lived long ago. You cannot feel Earth moving, so how would you know that it rotates on its axis? People long ago thought Earth did not move, so the explanation for the sun rising in the east and moving across the sky to set in the west was that the sun was traveling around Earth, and not the other way around.

Ancient astronomers did know that stars and planets moved differently. The stars seem to rotate around a fixed point high in the sky, but they do not change position relative to each other. The planets, on the other hand, move across the sky, from one constellation to another. Some cultures accounted for this difference by imagining a system where the sun and planets traveled in concentric circles around Earth, while the fixed stars were on the inside of a dome-shaped "lid" that rotated once each day.

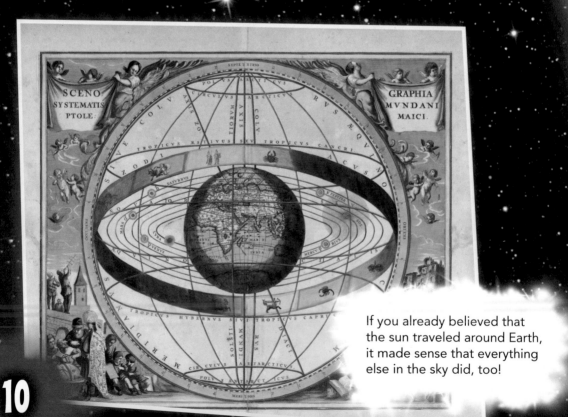

If you already believed that the sun traveled around Earth, it made sense that everything else in the sky did, too!

In the second century CE, Ptolemy's *Almagest* drew on the work of past astronomers to solidify his version of the universe. The moon was seen as orbiting closest to Earth, followed by Mercury and Venus, and then the sun. Beyond that were the other planets in the correct order. However, it was difficult to make this system match up exactly with the observations of astronomers.

GOING AGAINST THE CHURCH

It took a long time for the heliocentric (sun-centered) model to be accepted. One problem was the Catholic Church, which strongly supported the geocentric (Earth-centered) model. Some scientists, such as Galileo, were persecuted for supporting heliocentrism.

In 1543, Nicolaus Copernicus (1473–1543) published a book that proposed a solution: what if Earth and other planets actually orbited the sun? His system was still not quite right because he thought the planets had circular orbits. They are actually elliptical, and once Johannes Kepler (1571–1630) figured this out, the heliocentric model worked a lot better.

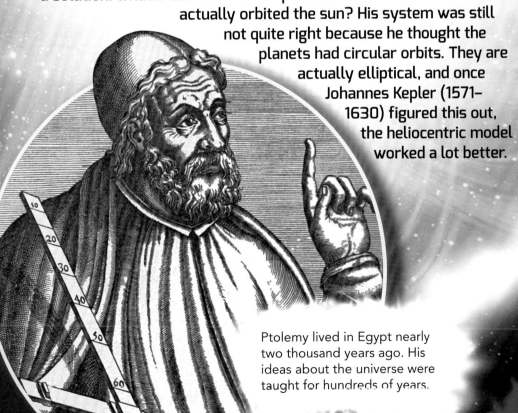

Ptolemy lived in Egypt nearly two thousand years ago. His ideas about the universe were taught for hundreds of years.

Chapter Two

STARS

Viewed from Earth, the stars look like beautiful twinkling pinpricks in the sky. However, the reality is very different. For a start, stars are enormous. They are giant, incredibly hot balls of hydrogen and helium, with nuclear reactions taking place in their cores to produce heat and light.

All stars have more or less the same ratio of elements inside them at the start: about three-quarters hydrogen and one-quarter helium. They also contain small amounts of other, heavier elements, such as oxygen, carbon, and nitrogen. Astronomers collectively call these heavier elements "metals." Depending on where they form and how old they are, stars can have more of these metals. Even so, it is a tiny percentage of the total. Our sun is considered to be a "metal-rich star," but those elements make up fewer than 3 percent of its mass.

NUCLEAR FUSION

Inside the core of a star, the temperature and pressure are high enough for nuclear fusion to take place. In a small-to-medium sized star, two hydrogen atoms fuse to form a deuterium atom. Then this merges with another hydrogen atom to create a form of helium. Finally two of those helium atoms merge to form a different type of helium atom. The process is exothermic, meaning that it releases energy. This energy takes the form of gamma rays that work their way to the surface of the star.

The structure of stars varies a little, depending on how large they are. However, all stars have a core, which is where the nuclear fusion takes place. The sun is a medium-sized star, and its core takes up about 20 percent of its diameter. Its core is about 170,000 miles (273,588 kilometers) across. The core is the hottest part of a star. Our sun's core is about 27,000,000 degrees Fahrenheit (15,000,000 degrees Celsius), but a larger star will have a bigger, hotter core.

Outside the core is a series of other layers. The convective and radiative zones allow the energy produced in the core to move outward. Outside them is the photosphere. This is the part of the star we see in visible light. Beyond that are the chromosphere and the corona.

Left: A lot of what we know about stars comes from studying our own star, the sun.

Right: This diagram shows the layers of the sun.

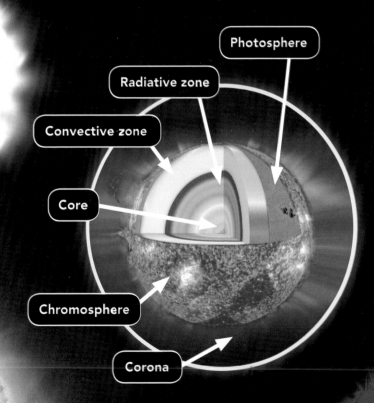

Photosphere

Radiative zone

Convective zone

Core

Chromosphere

Corona

Types of Stars

Astronomers classify stars based on a number of different characteristics. Aside from very young and very old stars (which we will look at later), as a general rule, the bigger a star is, the hotter and brighter it is. There are seven main types of stars: O, B, A, F, G, K, and M. The O and B stars are big and very bright, but fairly rare. At the other end of the scale, M stars are small, dim, and very common. Our sun is a type G star. Big stars can burn incredibly brightly; a type O star might only be sixty times the mass of the sun, but it could still be more than a million times as bright.

Stars can appear to be different colors, based on their surface temperatures. Big stars, such as O and B stars, will appear blue or bluish-white. Small, dim K and M stars will appear orange or red. Our sun is somewhere in the middle—a type of star called a yellow dwarf.

Some older stars do not follow the same pattern. For example, the star Betelgeuse, in the constellation of Orion, is a red star, but it is huge, as well as being one of the brightest stars in the sky. It is a type of star called a red giant. It has used up the fuel in its core and its outer layers have expanded. As they expand, these older stars become cooler and dimmer, which is why the star appears red instead of blue. Eventually, Betelgeuse will probably explode as a supernova.

This photograph shows thousands of yellow-white stars, like our sun, along with bright red stars near the end of their lives and younger blue stars.

Betelgeuse

Betelgeuse has a clear orange-red color when seen from Earth. Rigel is a giant blue star.

Rigel

WHAT IS THE SUN?

It seems obvious that our sun is a star, but people in ancient times thought the sun and stars were two different types of objects. Seen from Earth, they certainly do not look alike. A few astronomers proposed that stars might be just like the sun, only really far away, but no one took them seriously. It was only in the nineteenth century that someone accurately measured the distance to a star, which allowed us to see that its size and brightness were similar to the sun.

15

Learning about Stars

The stars are too far away and too hot to visit. Looking at the stars is fascinating, but there are limits to how much we can learn from this, even with the most powerful telescopes available. However, the energy that stars give out comes in many forms, and visible light is only one of them. Astronomers today use all the types of energy to find out more about stars. There are a range of different telescopes, on Earth and in space, which can detect the different types of energy.

Stars and other objects in space give off radio waves, which can be received by radio telescopes. The precise frequency given off by a star or other object can give clues as to what it is made of. Infrared telescopes pick up the infrared radiation (heat) emitted by objects and dust that cannot be seen by the human eye. Infrared telescopes have been used to find stars being born, as well as planets orbiting distant stars. X-ray telescopes can pick up extremely hot objects like stars, and have been used to find black holes. Using an ultraviolet detector can tell us a lot about a star's chemical make-up, as well as its temperature and density.

This spectrometer is part of the SOFIA mission, which uses a modified Boeing jet to carry a telescope and other instruments.

Gamma rays cannot penetrate Earth's atmosphere, so spacecraft like INTEGRAL orbit above the atmosphere to make observations.

Since 1990, astronomers have had another useful tool for studying stars. Telescopes in space have a big advantage over telescopes on Earth: they do not have to peer through Earth's thick atmosphere. The gases in our atmosphere can make images blurry and distort other types of signals, and the weather often interferes. Telescopes in space, such as the Spitzer Space Telescope, do not have these problems. They have made some amazing discoveries.

SPECTROMETERS

One of the most useful tools in astronomy is the spectrometer. A spectrometer takes the light collected by a telescope and splits it into its different colors. Astronomers can use this information to find out an object's temperature and mass, and calculate what direction it is moving and how quickly. Spectrometers can even help astronomers figure out what a star is made of.

17

Chapter Three

THE LIFE AND DEATH OF STARS

Stars are not alive in the same way that animals and plants are. However, we often use words such as "birth," "life," and "death" when we talk about stars. This is because they follow a progression that we often call a "life cycle." Over the course of millions or billions of years, they are formed, they change, and eventually they "die"—an event that can be marked with a slow burning out or a spectacular explosion.

A star begins its life in a giant cloud of gas and dust called a nebula, or sometimes a molecular cloud or stellar nursery. These clouds can be hundreds of light years across, containing enough raw materials to make thousands of stars. These raw materials are mainly hydrogen and helium, with small amounts of heavier elements. The force of gravity pulling in, combined with the force of the molecules pushing out, keeps the nebula in balance.

Nebulae are often named for their shapes. Some people think the Witch Head nebula looks like a fairytale character.

Then eventually, something happens to upset the balance. An encounter with another nebula or a star, or a nearby explosion, could make the nebula start collapsing in on itself. As it collapses, it breaks into smaller and smaller clumps, each with roughly the mass of a star. These clumps of gas start heating up and then form protostars.

After that, one of two things could happen. If there is enough mass in the protostar, it can reach temperatures of millions of degrees in its core. This temperature allows the chemical process of fusion to begin. However, some protostars do not have enough mass to get hot enough for fusion to start. They become what are known as brown dwarfs, and slowly cool down over the next few billion years.

This photograph of the North American nebula, taken by an infrared telescope, shows clusters of new stars forming.

THE STUFF OF SPACE

Though we often think of space as a vacuum, it is not completely empty. It is made up of a mixture of gas and dust that we call the interstellar medium (ISM). It is the ISM that eventually collapses and forms a nebula where stars can form.

Going Out with a Bang

Once a star begins to release energy, it is known as a main sequence star. A star with a similar mass to our own sun will stay in main sequence for about ten billion years. During that time, chemical reactions in its core will fuse hydrogen atoms together to form helium, but eventually the star will run out of fuel. When this happens, the core starts to contract and get hotter. Eventually it becomes hot enough for the helium to fuse and form carbon. The star's outer layers expand, and as they expand, they cool down and become less bright. The star is now called a red giant.

This dusty red cloud, called Puppis A, is all that remains of a supernova that took place about 3,700 years ago.

When the helium in the core is exhausted, the outer layers of the star drift away. It ends up with a gaseous shell, called a planetary nebula, surrounding the dying core. The core cools and dims, becoming a white dwarf. Eventually it stops shining and is then called a black dwarf.

Stars with significantly more mass than our sun follow a different path after they reach main sequence. Although they have a lot more fuel than smaller stars, they use it up much more quickly. Once this happens, the star becomes a red supergiant, with a helium core surrounded by a shell of cooling, expanding gas. In the core, chemical reactions create heavier and heavier elements, until the star can no longer extract any energy from the process. Its own gravity causes it to collapse, and the core heats up to billions of degrees Fahrenheit before exploding in a supernova. The explosion sends huge amounts of energy and matter out into space.

The giant star Eta Carinae burns its fuel so quickly that it is one million times as bright as our sun. Astronomers think that it will explode as a supernova soon.

SUPERNOVA LEFTOVERS

When a dying star explodes, it leaves behind the remains of its core. Depending on how massive the original star was, this core can turn into either a neutron star or a black hole. Both of these objects are extremely dense. A single teaspoon full of a neutron star's material, for example, would weigh about 1.1 billion tons (one billion metric tons)!

In this photograph of the remains of a supernova, you can see a dense neutron star glowing brightly at the center of the dust and gas clouds left by the explosion.

Studying Stars

In the past thirty years or so, improvements in technology and the launch of several space telescopes have meant that our knowledge of stars has grown by leaps and bounds. In addition to returning amazing images of nebulae, supernovae, and distant galaxies, these telescopes are allowing scientists to peer into the farthest corners of the universe. They are discovering some amazing things.

In 2007, astronomers scanning the universe for ultraviolet light discovered that a well-known star, called Mira, actually has a long tail, like a comet. Mira is a red giant, an older star that is starting to lose its surface material. As it hurtles through space, this tail, made up of carbon, oxygen, and other elements, streams out behind it.

In 2014, a team of researchers in Australia discovered that one star was older than any other known star. It is in the Milky Way galaxy, only about six thousand light years from Earth, and the astronomers estimate that it is 13.6 billion years old—nearly as old as the universe itself. They were able date it by scanning to see how much iron was present in the star. The older the star, the less iron it has.

A second discovery in 2014 was of the largest yellow star discovered —one of the ten largest stars we know of. Its diameter is more than 1,300 times larger than the sun's, and it is part of a double star system. Its partner star is so close that they actually touch!

Spacecraft such as the Chandra X-ray Observatory send back spectacular images. This shows an x-ray image of the supernova remains of Puppis A.

Top: Scientists hope to study Mira's tail to learn more about the star's life.

Bottom: Radio telescopes such as the Very Large Array in New Mexico can peer into the depths of space.

SEEING INTO THE PAST

The farthest known galaxy is more than thirteen billion light years away. This means that it takes thirteen billion years for its light to reach us. To put it another way, the light that astronomers are seeing now was actually emitted thirteen billion years ago. For all we know, the galaxy may not even exist anymore, but we will not know until the light finishes its long journey to the Milky Way!

Chapter Four

GALAXIES

Up until the 1920s, most astronomers believed that all the stars in the universe were contained in the Milky Way. However, since the invention of telescopes, astronomers had been cataloging what they called "nebulae," meaning "clouds." These objects might appear star-like to the naked eye, but through a telescope they are fuzzy and indistinct. A few astronomers speculated that some of these nebulae might actually be other galaxies, too far away to see clearly. They were right.

Now we know—or at least, we can estimate—that there between 100 billion and 200 billion galaxies in the universe. Since its launch in 1990, the Hubble Space Telescope has proved to be extremely useful at finding galaxies. In 2004, the telescope took a million-second exposure in a small area of the constellation Fornax. Astronomers were able to count ten thousand galaxies in the resulting image. In 2012, they looked again at a narrower portion of the field, but this time using upgraded instruments, and found even more galaxies.

Galaxies are not spread randomly throughout the universe; they clump together in groups. The Milky Way is part of a group of several dozen galaxies known as the Local Group. In turn, this group is part of the Virgo Supercluster, which contains at least one hundred groups and clusters of galaxies. In 2014, scientists discovered that even the Virgo Supercluster is part of a much larger grouping, the Laniakea Supercluster. All of its galaxies are being pulled toward a patch of space called the Great Attractor.

GALAXY WITHIN A GALAXY?

The closest galaxy to the Milky Way is actually inside it! In 2003, astronomers discovered the Canis Major Dwarf Galaxy by analyzing infrared images of the Milky Way. Those images showed the cool red M-type stars of Canis Major, which would otherwise be hard to see. At one point in the distant past, the Milky Way swallowed up the smaller galaxy, and now its stars are part of the Milky Way.

Aside from the Canis Major Dwarf galaxy and the Milky Way's other satellite galaxies, our nearest major galactic neighbor is the Andromeda galaxy, about 2.5 million light years away.

Types of Galaxies

Galaxies come in a huge range of sizes: the smallest dwarf galaxies may have only a few thousand stars, while the largest galaxies contain an estimated 100 trillion stars. On this scale, the Milky Way falls in the middle, with anywhere from 100 to 400 billion stars. Galaxies also come in a range of different shapes. The three basic galaxy shapes are elliptical, spiral, and irregular.

Elliptical galaxies are shaped like slightly squished spheres. From Earth, since we can see them in only two dimensions, they look like oval discs. They appear brightest at the center, then gradually becoming dimmer the farther out you go. They are classified based on how squished they are. An E0 galaxy is nearly a perfect circle. At the other end of the scale, an E7 galaxy is flattened.

A spiral galaxy has a bulge at the center, surrounded by a flat disc, a little like Saturn and its rings. The bulge at the center is made up mainly of older stars, and the disc contains younger stars, along with gas and dust. The arm shapes in the disc give spiral galaxies their name. Some spiral galaxies are called "barred spirals." In a barred spiral galaxy, the arms do not come out directly from the central bulge. Instead, there is a straight bar running through the center of the galaxy, and the arms come out from that.

The last type of galaxy is an irregular galaxy. These have a lot of gas and dust but no particular shape or structure, and they make up an estimated one-fourth of all galaxies. Some irregular galaxies probably used to be spiral or elliptical, but were deformed by gravity from other galaxies.

LENTICULAR GALAXIES

A fourth type of galaxy, the lenticular galaxy, is really just a halfway point between an elliptical galaxy and a spiral galaxy. These galaxies have a central bulge and a thin disc, like a spiral galaxy, but they have no spiral structure. They are shaped a little like a lens, which is how they get their name.

Top: The spiral galaxy M101 is estimated to contain at least one trillion stars.

Right: This galaxy began life as a spiral galaxy, but as it ages it will turn into an elliptical galaxy. At the moment it is in the in-between stage and is known as a lenticular galaxy.

27

Black Holes

Astronomers believe that at the center of nearly all galaxies, including the Milky Way, there is a black hole. A black hole is not really a hole: holes are empty, and black holes are not empty. They are areas where there is a huge amount of matter squished into a very small space. Since they are so incredibly dense, they exert a huge gravitational field. It is so strong that nothing can escape it.

Most black holes are formed when a massive star dies. Our sun is not big enough to turn into a black hole, but a much bigger star will explode in a supernova after it uses up its fuel. Part of the dying star is blasted off into space, and the remainder collapses under the force of its own gravity to form a black hole. These are known as stellar mass black holes.

The black holes at the center of galaxies are much bigger—so much bigger, in fact, that they are called supermassive black holes. They have a mass equal to more than one million suns. Astronomers are trying to figure out how supermassive black holes form. One recent theory is that they start out small, but grow and grow as more matter falls into them.

Early theories about black holes were based on the work of the great physicist Albert Einstein (1879–1955).

Studying black holes is tricky. Nothing, not even light, can escape them, so we have no way to "see" them. We cannot even use x-rays or other forms of energy to see them. However, we can infer their presence by looking for their effect on other nearby objects. For example, if a star or cloud of gas and dust passes near a black hole, its matter will be drawn toward the black hole.

This artist's drawing shows a black hole named Cygnus X-1, which is pulling matter from the blue star next to it.

POINT OF NO RETURN

Black holes are surrounded by a boundary known as the event horizon. Once something falls inside the event horizon, it can never escape. Even time is distorted near the event horizon. To an outside observer, something falling into the black hole would appear to move more and more slowly, but never reach it.

Galaxies on the Move

In the first half of the twentieth century, scientists wrestled with the concept of the universe. Has it always been there, or was there a time when it did not exist? Does it go on forever, or does it have an edge somewhere? These are incredibly difficult questions to answer, and we still do not know for sure. Improved technology has helped scientists get closer to the answers.

One of the key breakthroughs was the discovery that galaxies do not stand still in space. In the 1920s, the astronomer Edwin Hubble (1889–1953) studied the spectra of light coming from distant galaxies. Objects that are moving away from us emit light that is shifted toward the red end of the spectrum. This phenomenon is a result of the Doppler Effect, the same thing that makes an ambulance's siren sound more high-pitched as it approaches you. The farther away a galaxy is, the more its light is red-shifted.

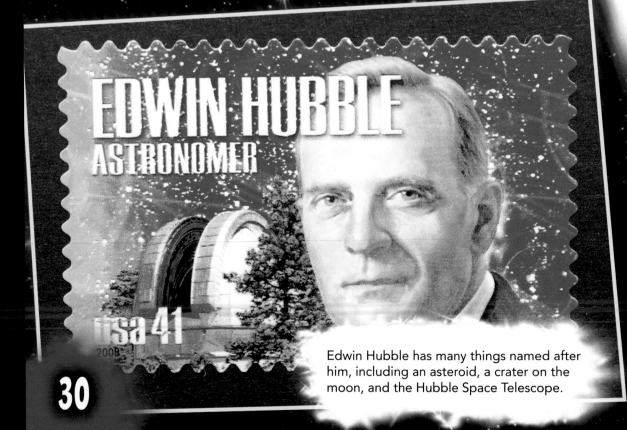

EDWIN HUBBLE
ASTRONOMER

usa 41

2008

Edwin Hubble has many things named after him, including an asteroid, a crater on the moon, and the Hubble Space Telescope.

Based on Hubble's discovery that galaxies are moving away from each other, astronomers came to the conclusion that the universe must be expanding. It is a little like a loaf of raisin bread rising in the oven: as it rises, the raisins (like galaxies) are caught up in the expanding dough and move away from each other. If the universe is expanding, then it must have been much smaller at some point in the past. That led to the concept of the Big Bang: the idea that the universe began as a single point before expanding rapidly.

BUCKING THE TREND

Although many galaxies are moving away from each other, the Milky Way and the Andromeda galaxy are actually moving toward each other. The force of the gravitational attraction between them is stronger than the force of the universe expanding. They will collide in about four billion years.

In 1963, a pair of astronomers discovered microwave radiation coming equally from all directions. They thought something was wrong with their antenna, but then realized that this was background radiation left over from the Big Bang. Scientists have studied this radiation to learn more about how the universe formed.

This "map" shows the oldest light in our universe, called the cosmic microwave background radiation. The colors show tiny temperature differences that indicate regions where the seeds of future stars and galaxies were found.

Chapter Five

DEEP SPACE MYSTERIES

There is a lot about the universe that we still do not understand, and new discoveries are always being made. One of the most useful discoveries was the existence of pulsars. In 1967, astronomers Jocelyn Bell (b. 1943) and Antony Hewish (b. 1924) picked up a mysterious radio emission from a point in the sky. It peaked every 1.33 seconds precisely. This sort of regularity is unusual, and some scientists thought it was communication from an intelligent life form.

Additional discoveries confirmed that Bell and Hewish had discovered the first pulsar. A pulsar is created after a supernova, when the exploding star does not have enough mass to become a black hole. Instead, the remains of the supernova collapse to form a neutron star. This neutron star is small and very dense, and when it starts to spin rapidly, it sends out powerful blasts of radiation, but only along the lines of its magnetic field.

More recent discoveries have shown that pulsars have a limited life span. They start off spinning incredibly quickly, but as they release more and more energy through their beams, they start to slow down. After ten to 100 million years, a pulsar will slow down enough that its beams shut off, and it becomes quiet.

Copies of this golden record were sent on Voyager 1 and Voyager 2, in case they are ever found by an alien civilization. The starburst shape at the bottom left shows the location of our solar system in relation to fourteen pulsars.

The twin beams of energy from a pulsar sweep around like the light from a lighthouse, keeping regular time.

LITTLE GREEN MEN

Bell and Hewish did not really believe that the signal they found was a message from another civilization, but they did consider the possibility. They named the signal LGM-1, which stood for "Little Green Men."

Pulsars are incredibly useful to astronomers. They spin with such regularity that they can be used as timers. They are also used to search for things called gravitational waves, which are like ripples in the fabric of space-time. When they pass through an object, these ripples make it shrink or stretch by a tiny amount. A group of scientists has recently proposed using the signals from pulsars as a sort of universal GPS system for any spacecraft navigating beyond our solar system.

Quasars

The mystery of quasars started in the 1960s, when astronomers looking at radio waves from stars found several small, incredibly bright objects that they could not explain. They called them quasi-stellar radio sources—"quasars" for short—and tried to find out what they actually were.

Over the next twenty years or so, astronomers argued over different theories about quasars. Some quasars were shown to be moving away from us at extremely fast speeds. Some were emitting as much light as an entire galaxy. Astronomers wondered if they could be caused by a black hole distorting gravity, or if they could be one end of a wormhole.

In the 1980s, astronomers began to agree that quasars were related to what is called an active galactic nucleus (AGN). Nucleus is just another word for the center of a galaxy, and some galaxies have centers that are active, meaning that they emit large amounts of radiation. The radiation can take the form of radio waves, visible light, x-rays, gamma rays, and more. The radiation is also highly variable. This means that it can change intensity in a short amount of time.

The best explanation for quasars seems to be that they are supermassive black holes at the centers of some galaxies. As material is pulled into the black hole, some of the matter is converted into energy, and it is this energy that we see. When there is no matter "feeding" the black hole, the jets of energy shut down. There is no matter entering the supermassive black hole at the center of the Milky Way, so our galaxy does not appear as a quasar.

The Hubble Space Telescope took this photograph of the first quasar ever to be identified. Its light has taken 2.5 billion years to reach us.

SEEING QUASARS

A quasar can easily be one hundred times brighter than the host galaxy that surrounds it. As a result of this, we cannot not take a photograph that shows both the quasar and the host galaxy—the galaxy is lost in the quasar's glare. It is only fairly recently that photographic technology has improved to the point where we can now detect a big enough range of brightnesses in a single image.

This artist's drawing shows energy being emitted from a quasar.

Dark Matter

Understanding gravity is important to understanding how the universe works. All objects with mass are attracted—through the force of gravity— to other objects. The greater the mass, the stronger the pull. It is gravity that keeps Earth in orbit around the sun and holds the Milky Way together.

Astronomers soon noticed a problem with gravity: there did not seem to be enough mass around to exert the gravitational force that could be observed. In the 1930s, an astronomer named Fritz Zwicky (1898–1974) was studying a far-off cluster of galaxies when he realized that if the only mass in the cluster was the galaxies themselves, then they were moving too fast for that amount of gravity to hold them together. He decided that there must be a lot of additional matter that we cannot see because it does not emit light.

This is a composite image showing a Hubble photograph of a galaxy cluster, with a map of the cluster's dark matter superimposed on it. The dark ring is where the dark matter is.

DARK ENERGY

In 1998, data from the Hubble Space Telescope showed that the expansion of the universe is accelerating. This surprised scientists, who thought that the force of gravity would eventually slow it down. One theory to explain acceleration is that the universe is full of something called "dark energy," which has the opposite effect of gravity, and pulls galaxies apart.

Top: The Large Hadron Collider is carrying out experiments that scientists hope will shed light on the mystery of dark matter.

Bottom: The Fermi Gamma-ray Space Telescope is looking for gamma rays being given off when dark matter particles decay.

Since then, scientists have tried to figure out the truth behind dark matter, and there are a lot of theories but no firm answers. There is evidence that the amount of dark matter in the universe is a lot higher than the amount of matter we can see. Other evidence shows that dark matter cannot be made up of protons and neutrons, like the matter we know of. It could be made up of a type of particle that we have not yet discovered.

Several projects searching for dark matter are underway. Some scientists are working on designing new types of detection tools that will allow them to detect dark matter particles. Other studies focus on detecting the effects of dark matter, for example, by looking for x-rays or gamma rays being given off when dark matter particles decay. Others collide beams of high-energy protons to look for dark matter particles in the results.

Chapter Six

WHAT COULD WE FIND?

Modern technology and tools like space telescopes are redefining astronomy, leading to an incredible expansion in what we know about the universe. Even so, there are so many questions that remain unanswered. What is dark matter? Will the universe continue to expand indefinitely? Is there intelligent life anywhere out there?

New discoveries come thick and fast. In 2013, data from the Planck space telescope showed that the universe is older than we had thought. This means that space and time are not expanding quite as fast as scientists had estimated. That same year, another team of scientists discovered a record-breaking cluster of quasars stretching four billion light years across. In 2014, researchers announced that they had found the first direct evidence for the dramatic expansion that happened just after the Big Bang.

This telescope at the south pole studies the cosmic microwave background radiation.

The Wilkinson Microwave Anisotropy Probe measured temperature differences in the heat left over from the Big Bang.

THE THIRST FOR KNOWLEDGE

Many arguments about money spent on astronomy miss out on the key thing driving most astronomers—the need to find answers. It is human nature to ask questions about how the universe was created and where we came from. With advances in technology, we are getting closer to being able to answer those questions.

Despite these discoveries, many people question why we spend so much time, effort, and money studying things that are billions of light years away. For example, it will cost nearly $9 billion to get the James Webb Space Telescope into orbit. With all of the problems our planet faces, some people wonder if that money could be better spent closer to home.

The truth is that research into space has benefits on Earth. Many technologies developed for astronomy have other useful applications. For example, the charge-coupled device that makes your smartphone work was originally developed for astronomy. GPS satellites rely on quasars and distant galaxies to determine their position and help you find your way. A computer language designed to control a telescope is now used to track packages during shipping.

Is There Anyone Out There?

One of the questions scientists have been trying to answer for decades is whether we are alone in the universe. Many scientists believe that given the incredible size of the universe, and the sheer number of stars with planets orbiting them, we would be naive to think that only Earth is home to living things. From a mathematical perspective, that view makes a lot of sense. However, proving it is another matter entirely.

The search for extraterrestrial intelligence (often called SETI) has been carried out over the years by government agencies, universities, and private companies. One of the main methods of searching has been by analyzing radio waves from outside the solar system. Our own civilization emits a lot of radiation through things like television broadcasts. The signals are easy to recognize as being artificial, and if we could find similar signals coming from space, it might be a sign of intelligent life. One new technique is using telescopes to search for alien laser signals. Lasers are a way of transmitting messages over huge distances, but the signals would be incredibly faint by the time they reached Earth.

If there is intelligent life elsewhere in the universe, these beings may be conducting their own version of SETI. What would happen if they found us? Some scientists have speculated that if an alien civilization is more advanced than ours, it might be able to destroy us. After all, in Earth's own history, when two cultures have met for the first time, the less-advanced culture has often been harmed. Some scientists think we should "lie low," and not try to alert other civilizations to our presence.

LIFE, BUT NOT AS WE KNOW IT

Life on Earth has evolved to take advantage of the conditions on our home planet. For example, all life we know of requires water, and there is plenty water on Earth. Plants and animals are adapted to the fairly narrow range of temperatures found on Earth. However in alien worlds, with other conditions, life might look very different.

The Allen Telescope Array in California was built to search for signals that might come from alien civilizations.

Exoplanets

One thing that could speed up the search for intelligent life is the discovery of planets orbiting distant stars. They are called exoplanets or extrasolar planets, and they are being discovered at an amazing rate. Since the first one was found in 1992, they have been popping up everywhere, and at the last count there were nearly two thousand of them. These exoplanets are too far away for us to visit with current technology, but in the distant future, we may be able to colonize them.

Planets do not emit light, and compared to stars, they are incredibly small, so we cannot directly see them with telescopes. One way to find exoplanets is by looking for tiny changes in a star's velocity, which are caused by the planet's gravity pulling at them. This technique is most useful for finding gas giants similar to Jupiter. Another technique is to look for changes in a star's light. If a planet passes in front of a star, it will block some of the light and make the star appear slightly dimmer. This is how the Kepler space telescope finds exoplanets.

Finding an exoplanet is just the first step. Astronomers need to then find out what it is made of, and whether it has things like an atmosphere or liquid water. One way of doing this is to study the exoplanet through the infrared portion of the electromagnetic spectrum, looking for chemical signatures of different elements. An experiment using the Keck Observatory in Hawaii was able to use spectroscopy to identify water molecules in the atmosphere of one exoplanet.

The Kepler mission has discovered a planet, Kepler-16b, that orbits two stars. In this artist's impression you can see the planet silhouetted against a small red dwarf star and a larger star.

THE GOLDILOCKS ZONE

Astronomers can gauge how habitable a planet might be by seeing how far it is from the star it orbits. If it is too close, the surface would be too hot, and any liquid water would evaporate into space. If it is too far away, it would be too cold, and the water would freeze. If a planet falls in the "just right" area—often called the Goldilocks zone—it is more likely to have liquid water on the surface.

The exoplanet Kepler-186f is the first Earth-size planet we have found that orbits its star within the "Goldilocks zone." Liquid water might exist there.

43

What's Next?

In 2013, an amazing milestone was reached when the Voyager 1 probe left the solar system behind and traveled into interstellar space. It is the only man-made object ever to leave the solar system, although it will be followed shortly by its partner, Voyager 2. Both probes are still sending back data about the conditions they encounter on their voyage into the universe.

As a result of the huge distances involved, the next breakthroughs in the study of the universe will come from telescopes on Earth, or from those in orbit around it. We are already getting great results from the Hubble, Spitzer, and Kepler space telescopes, as well as the Chandra X-ray Observatory. The James Webb Space Telescope, which uses infrared radiation, is set to join them in orbit around Earth.

Scientists are currently investigating a huge range of topics. Research into new technologies is keeping pace, bringing telescopes and other tools that are much more sensitive than before. The search for dark matter and dark energy continues, and there are many studies looking at energy that will give us clues to conditions just after the Big Bang. Since the launch of Kepler, the study of exoplanets has become a very popular area of research. There is still a lot to be learned, even within our own galaxy.

The James Webb Space Telescope will study how stars and galaxies form, search for light from the first stars, and try to find out more about planetary systems.

CAN WE GO THERE?

Unless there is an incredible breakthrough in technology, it is unlikely that humans will ever visit another star. The nearest star, Alpha Centauri, is 4.3 light years away. At the maximum speed of a space shuttle, it would take 165,000 years to get there. Traveling outside the Milky Way would take even longer. The nearest large galaxy, Andromeda, is 2.5 million light years away, so even if we could travel at the speed of light—which we cannot—it would take 2.5 million years to reach it.

GLOSSARY

asterisms Groups of stars that appear to make a shape or pattern when seen from Earth.

astronomers People who study planets, stars, and other objects beyond Earth.

atmosphere The layer of gases surrounding a planet.

atoms The smallest possible units of a chemical element. Atoms are the basis of all matter in the universe.

Big Bang A point in time in the distant past when the universe began with a huge explosion.

black holes Dense regions or bodies in space with gravity so strong that light and matter cannot escape them.

constellation A recognizable pattern of stars that makes up one of the eighty-eight regions of the sky designated by astronomers.

dark matter A type of matter that is believed to exist, which cannot be seen but still exerts a gravitational force.

ecliptic The apparent path of the sun, as seen from Earth against the background stars.

elliptical Shaped like a slightly squished circle.

exoplanets Planets that orbit a star other than our sun.

galaxies Groups of billions of stars and other matter held together by gravity.

gamma rays High-energy electromagnetic radiation. Some objects in space produce gamma rays.

gravity The force that pulls all objects toward each other.

infrared radiation A type of electromagnetic energy with a long wavelength, which cannot be seen as visible light.

light years Units of distance equal to the distance light can travel in one year, about six trillion miles (9.46 trillion km).

mass A measure of how much matter is in an object.

microwave A type of high-frequency radio wave. It can be used to send information over long distances.

nebula A cloud of gas and dust in space. Stars are formed in some nebulae.

neutron star A small, incredibly dense type of star that forms after a supernova.

nuclear fusion A chemical process in which the nuclei of two or more atoms fuse into a more massive nucleus. This process releases a huge amount of energy.

orbiting When one body in space travels on a curved path around another object, such as a moon orbiting a planet.

particle One of the tiniest units of matter we know of. Atoms are made up of particles such as protons, neutrons, and electrons.

pulsars Types of rapidly rotating neutron stars that send out regularly timed pulses of energy.

quasars Objects found in the centers of some galaxies that emit huge amounts of energy.

radiation The waves of energy sent out by sources of heat or light.

radio waves Very low-frequency type of electromagnetic waves.

spectrometer A tool used for measuring wavelengths of light by spreading radiation into an ordered sequence.

supernovae Rare and very bright objects that result from the explosion of a massive star.

ultraviolet light A type of electromagnetic energy with a short wavelength, which cannot be seen as visible light.

universe All matter and energy that exist.

x-ray A type of very high-energy electromagnetic radiation. X-rays can penetrate though many kinds of solid material.

FOR MORE INFORMATION

Books

Aguilar, David A. *Space Encyclopedia: A Tour of Our Solar System and Beyond.* Washington, D.C.: National Geographic Kids, 2013.

Einspruch, Andrew. *Mysteries of the Universe: How Astronomers Explore Space* (National Geographic Science Chapters). Washington, D.C.: National Geographic Children's Books, 2006.

Farndon, John. *What Do We Know About Stars and Galaxies?* (Earth, Space, & Beyond). Chicago, IL: Heinemann-Raintree, 2011.

Miller, Ron. *Seven Wonders Beyond the Solar System* (Seven Wonders). Minneapolis, MN: Twenty-First Century Books, 2011.

Snedden, Robert. *How Do Scientists Explore Space?* (Earth, Space, & Beyond). Chicago, IL: Heinemann-Raintree, 2012.

Thomas, Isabel. *Stars and Galaxies* (Astronaut Travel Guides). Chicago, IL: Heinemann-Raintree, 2013.

Websites

Due to the changing nature of Internet links, Rosen Publishing has developed an online list of websites related to the subject of this book. This site is updated regularly. Please use this link to access the list:

http://www.rosenlinks.com/SSS/Solar

INDEX